"Teachers plant the seeds of knowledge that last a lifetime."

This book was generously
donated in memory of

Kristen Lee Meister,
a beloved educator, colleague,
mentor & friend.

KATE

A Magic School for Girls Chapter Book

A.M. Luzzader

Illustrated by Anna Hilton

Published by Knowledge Forest Press
P.O. Box 6331
Logan, UT 84341

Ebook ISBN-13: 978-1-949078-36-7
Paperback ISBN-13: 978-1-949078-35-0

Cover design by Sleepy Fox Studio

Editing by Chadd VanZanten

Interior illustrations by Anna Hilton

CONTENTS

CHAPTER 1
ART BEFORE BREAKFAST

Kate knew she didn't have a lot of time. She was already dressed in her school uniform, which consisted of a crisp white shirt, a dark skirt, a necktie, and special shoes. However, she still needed to eat breakfast before she walked with her two best friends to Annette McGill's School of Magic for Magically Gifted Girls.

Kate tucked her short black hair behind her ears and then put on her artist apron and stood in front of her art easel. She was a little nervous about being late, but she couldn't help it. She had to make a little art this morning. Art was Kate's favorite thing--painting and drawing and sculpting clay. Kate loved creating things.

Perhaps that was why she liked going to Annette McGill's School of Magic for Magically Gifted Girls, which was also known as Miss Annie's Magic School. It was a special private school where girls who believed in magic were trained to be witches. Kate was now eight years old, old enough to attend Miss Annie's Magic School, and she knew that magic could be used to create lots of things, including art.

Kate dreamed of someday using her magic skills to create incredible art pieces. She knew one day she would be able to combine art and magic, but for now, she was happy to use ordinary paints and paint-brushes.

Kate's latest painting was of a unicorn galloping under a rainbow. Kate added a dab of purple to the unicorn's flowing mane. Then she added some fluffy clouds to the sky. She was going to add some glitter to the painting, but just then her mother called out to her.

"Kate," her mother said from the kitchen, "hurry and eat your breakfast, or you'll be late for school."

"Okay," Kate called back. "I'll be down in just a minute."

"Are you painting again?" Kate's mom asked.

"You know you're supposed to wait until after school to work on your painting."

Kate slipped off her apron and put her brushes in a cup of water. "Sorry," she said. "I just couldn't wait to work on it. I really like this one."

Kate's mom came down the hall and poked her

head into Kate's room. "I have to admit," her mom said, "it's very good!"

"Thanks, Mom," said Kate, smiling. "I knew you'd like it."

"I'd like it even more if you would eat breakfast and get to school," said her mom. "I made you a special breakfast today."

Kate and her mom headed for the kitchen. "What is it?" Kate asked.

"Scrambled eggs, muffins, and a dragon's wort smoothie," said her mom.

Kate paused in the hallway. "Dragon's wort?"

"Yes, Bailey's mom told me it helps with magic."

Kate made a face and wrinkled her nose. "I don't think I'll like that."

"Will you try it?" asked her mom. "I think it tastes pretty good."

"Do I have to?" Kate asked.

Her mom frowned. "I guess not. I'll just give it to your dad."

"Do I have to eat the eggs, too? I don't really like eggs very much."

"What will you eat?" her mom asked.

"I'll eat the muffin," said Kate.

Her mom sighed.

"You're a very picky eater, Kate. Eggs have a lot of nutrients in them. And I know how much you love magic. I was hoping this smoothie would give you a boost in your class."

Kate made a face as they entered the kitchen and she saw the smoothie. "It doesn't look good," said Kate. "I wouldn't like it."

"You don't know that for sure," replied her mom, hoping that Kate's picky eating was something she would grow out of.

Kate quickly ate the muffin and then dashed outside to meet her two best friends, Bailey and Julie, so they could all walk to school together. Julie had long blond hair, and Bailey had black curly hair and glasses. Of course, both Julie and Bailey were also wearing the required school uniform. In fact, Julie and Bailey both liked the uniforms because it showed they were students at Miss Annie's Magic School.

However, Kate didn't like the uniform very much. She found it rather plain. Kate wished she could wear brightly colored clothes and different shoes every day. She liked hats and jewelry and scarves. Kate was an artist, after all, and she thought artists should wear unique and interesting outfits.

The three friends stopped in front of the entrance of the school building, a large old mansion of red brick. Vines with deep green leaves climbed the walls. It was a tall building with lots of fancy windows, towers, and an iron weather vane with a bat on top. The school may have been a little spooky, but it was also beautiful.

"Have fun in class," said Kate to her friends.

"You too," said Julie.

"We'll see you at recess," said Bailey.

Julie and Bailey were in Miss Betsy Bumble's class that year. However, even though Kate was best friends with Julie and Bailey and they were all the same age, Kate was not in Miss Betsy's class. Kate was in Mr. Jack Jasper's class.

On their first day of Miss Annie's Magic School, the three friends had walked to the school together, but then Julie and Bailey had left to go to their class. Kate didn't know anyone else at the school. She felt a little bit left out that her two friends were in a class together.

As she had walked sadly to her class that day, Miss Annie herself, the director of the school, spotted Kate in the hallway. Miss Annie was a tall, elegant witch. She was thin, with a long face, long nose, and long, beautiful, snow-white hair. Miss Annie wore a black, close-fitting witch's dress, and the tall witch's hat Miss Annie wore showed that she was a master witch, who had completed years of training and graduated from a magic university. All the girls at Miss Annie's Magic School hoped they could be master witches someday, too.

On that first day of class, Miss Annie approached

Kate and said, "It's not easy when your two best friends are in a different class, is it?"

Kate gasped quietly. How did Miss Annie know what Kate was feeling? She hadn't told anyone that she was sad about it. How did Miss Annie know? It must be magic, Kate thought.

"I would like it better if I were in the same class as Bailey and Julie," said Kate.

Miss Annie smiled. "Yes, I understand," she said. "It's natural to want to be with your friends."

"Could you make it so that I can be in Miss Betsy's class, too?" Kate asked. Miss Annie was the director of the school after all.

"Yes," said Miss Annie, "I certainly could."

"Oh!" cried Kate. "Thank you, Miss Annie!"

"Not so fast," said Miss Annie. "I said I could transfer you to Miss Betsy's class, but that wouldn't be fair to you, Kate. Mr. Jack is a fantastic teacher and there are many wonderful students in his class for you to make friends with. I think there's a reason you've been placed in Mr. Jack's class. Now you just have to figure out what it is."

Kate had gone to the class, wondering if she really was meant to be there, and wondering if it would really end up better than being in the same class as her two best friends.

CHAPTER 2
MR. JACK JASPER

When Kate walked into her classroom, she saw many students but no teacher, so she walked over to a girl with pigtails and a bowtie.

"Where's our teacher?" Kate asked.

The girl pointed at the ceiling. Kate looked up and saw Mr. Jack Jasper for the first time. He was hanging upside-down from the ceiling like a bat. He was wrapped in a black cape and in his mouth, he wore a set of plastic vampire teeth. Mr. Jack winked at Kate, but he didn't say anything. Kate laughed and found her desk. When the bell rang for class to start, Mr. Jack jumped off from the ceiling, spread the cape like a pair of bat wings, flipped over, and landed on his feet in front of the class.

The students didn't know what to think of this, so they began to clap.

Mr. Jack bowed. He had a jolly round face, happy blue eyes, and a big, friendly smile.

"Thank you, thank you!" he said. "Welcome to your first day at Annette McGill's School of Magic for Magically Gifted Girls! I am Mr. Jack Jasper. You may call me Mr. Jack. In my class, you will learn interesting and engaging feats such as how to sleep upside down while hanging from the ceiling, and making potions that will allow you to do everything from seeing through walls to walking through walls!"

The students ooo'ed and ahh'ed. Mr. Jack talked with such excitement Kate thought it was more like a magic show or circus rather than a school class. She started feeling slightly less gloomy.

The kids clapped again.

"You're too kind," said Mr. Jack. "Oops, hold on." The teeth in his mouth had come loose and had almost fallen out. "There that's better," said Mr. Jack, taking the teeth out of his mouth. He tossed the plastic teeth into the air and they exploded into a mini firework. Then, he took off his cape and folded it into a chair!

Kate was completely amazed by Mr. Jack. He

wasn't just a wizard; he was funny and entertaining, too! She began to think maybe it was okay to be in a class without her two best friends.

Mr. Jack told the students all the interesting things that the students would be learning that year-- how to fly on broomsticks, grab and fetch spells, and how to make magical potions.

"Potions are my specialty," said Mr. Jack. "I am an expert on all potions, concoctions, and elixirs. Soon you will know a lot about potions, too!"

After he'd removed his cape and turned it into a chair, Mr. Jack put on a cone-shaped hat covered with purple spirals, golden stars, and silver moons. It was a sign that he had been to a magical university and become a master wizard, just like Miss Annie was a master witch. Mr. Jack had majored in potions, and so the class would include lots of lessons on potions.

"We will learn about invisibility potions, friendship potions, and potions for walking through walls!" cried Mr. Jack, waving his arms and pacing all around the class. "I will even teach you a potion that will turn your skin green!"

Kate turned to the girl with pigtails and a bowtie and whispered, "I wonder if that is why everyone thinks witches have green skin!"

The girl laughed, and Kate laughed, too.

"I'm Whitney," the girl whispered.

"I'm Kate. It's nice to meet you."

Miss Annie was right! Kate was already making new friends. She felt rather happy.

"Mr. Jack seems really fun," said Whitney.

Kate nodded. Mr. Jack did seem fun and Whitney seemed very nice, too.

But then the smile disappeared from Mr. Jack's face. He stared at the class. "Now," he said, "I don't want you thinking that spells are just for fun and games. There are many important and serious potions that you'll need to learn."

Kate's eyes grew wide as she listened.

"There are healing potions and learning potions and potions that will help you know what's right and wrong. Some of these potions are very, very complicated and you may find them difficult to learn."

The class was quiet now. Mr. Jack wore a serious expression. Kate thought maybe the class wouldn't be fun after all.

But then Mr. Jack broke into his smile once more. "But mostly, this class will be lots of fun!" He stretched out his arms and a wild swarm of tiny fireworks burst in the air above the desks.

The students laughed and clapped.

"Students, do you know what you must do if you want to be good at magic?"

The students were silent, waiting for the answer.

"You have to pocus on it!"

A few students laughed.

"Get it?" said Mr. Jack. "Pocus! As in hocus pocus!"

More of the students laughed, but some of them only groaned.

"I know, I know," said Mr. Jack. "It's a corny joke,

but it's my favorite one. Now! Everyone get out your magic wands."

Kate grabbed her wand from her backpack.

"Now stand up," said Mr. Jack. "And repeat after me. I will be a good student. I will try my hardest. And most of all, I promise to tell Mr. Jack that he is the best teacher I've ever had! Now zap yourself with your wands to seal the deal."

The students laughed and repeated what Mr. Jack had said before playfully aiming their wands at themselves. Kate was already having so much fun, she couldn't imagine being in any other class.

CHAPTER 3
POTION PROBLEMS

Just like Miss Annie had said, there were many other wonderful students in Kate's class, and she made new friends quickly. There was Whitney, the girl Kate met on the first day of class. Later Whitney and Kate made friends with Jordan, a girl with red hair and big eyeglasses. But Kate was still best friends with Bailey and Julie, and they walked to school every day.

One day, as the three friends were walking to school, Bailey said, "I'm so excited for today. I can hardly wait for class."

Bailey was always excited for magic class. She was one of the smartest girls at school. Sometimes other kids at school even teased her about it.

"What are you so excited about?" Kate asked

Bailey "Is there something different happening or are you just excited for a regular day of school?"

"Julie knows," said Bailey. "Our class is learning something new today. It's going to be awesome."

Julie asked, "We're learning something new today?"

"Yes," said Bailey. "Don't you remember? Today is our introduction to flying broomsticks!"

"Our class is learning about flying broomsticks next week," said Kate. "Do you think it will be fun or scary?"

"Oh, don't worry," said Bailey. "Julie and I will tell you all about it! Right, Julie?"

"I'd forgotten about that," said Julie. "For me it will be very scary. I have a fear of heights."

"I'll try to help you," said Bailey, patting Julie gently on the back.

"I'm looking forward to learning to fly on broomsticks," said Kate.

"So what is your class studying then?" asked Bailey as she adjusted her pink glasses.

"We're starting a whole section on potions today," said Kate. "It sounds super fun! We have to learn some boring potions, too, but Mr. Jack promised that if we pay attention and do our homework, he'll teach us some extra fun potions and elixirs."

"I heard that Mr. Jack is really good with potions," said Bailey.

"He is," said Kate. "He's a master wizard and his specialty is potions."

"Then you will need to tell us everything you learn about the potions," said Bailey.

Kate knew Bailey wasn't just saying that. Bailey loved to learn new things. Kate was pretty sure that Bailey did homework just for fun.

"Okay, I will," said Kate.

When she got to class, Mr. Jack handed her a pair of safety goggles. "Safety first," he said.

Kate put the goggles on and tucked her hair behind her ears. She was surprised about the safety goggles, but once she thought about it, it made a lot of sense. Witches had to be careful or things could get out of hand fast. Like the time Bailey's sister Kiara had turned their dog, Woofer, into a baby hippo.

But grown-up witches who had graduated from a magical university were always very safe. So, it really shouldn't have been a surprise that they'd wear safety goggles to protect their eyes from splashes or unexpected explosions.

Their desks were arranged into pairs that day and in the middle of each pair of desks was a magical flame and a small cauldron for boiling potions.

"Who wants to bounce like a rubber ball?" asked Mr. Jack. "Who wants to be able to jump super high and bounce through the air? Well, I hope all of you do, because the Uber Jumpy Rubbery Blubbery potion is what we're learning today. You'll all be bouncing off the walls, and for once, your teacher won't complain!"

Kate and Whitney, who were partners that day, smiled at each other. Mr. Jack had made potions sound super fun.

"But you'll need to follow all the instructions carefully in order to make the potion," said Mr. Jack.

On their desks were also a recipe card and ingredients. Kate picked up the recipe card and read through it.

"Frog jelly, grasshopper juice, jumping beans, bunny sweat, and flea eggs," Kate read.

"The ingredients are all from things that hop and jump," said Whitney. "I wonder what this potion will taste like."

Just then, a very concerned look crossed Kate's face.

```
┌─────────────────────────────────────┐
│               Recipe                │
│  ─────────────────────────────────  │
│   Frog Jelly                        │
│   Grasshopper Juice                 │
│   Jumping Beans                     │
│   Bunny Sweat                       │
│   Flea Eggs                         │
│                                     │
└─────────────────────────────────────┘
```

"Is something the matter, Kate?" asked Whitney.

Kate had just realized something.

It was something she hadn't thought of before.

She was pretty sure she would have to drink this potion!

After they cooked up all these weird ingredients into a magic potion, she knew she'd never be able to drink it. Kate didn't even like regular old scrambled eggs, so she wouldn't dream of eating a flea egg or any of the other icky things.

"Oh, nothing's the matter," replied Kate. "Just concentrating on the ingredients."

Even though Kate was suddenly feeling very worried, she and Whitney followed the recipe closely. They measured out the ingredients in the amounts on the recipe card. Then mixed them into the cauldron in the order that the recipe showed.

As they combined the ingredients and said the magic words, a gooey purple liquid formed, and sparks and smoke emerged from the cauldron.

Just then, Mr. Jack came to check on Kate and Whitney. "Yes! Yes!" he said with a large grin. "Your potion is just the right shade of purple!" Then he dipped his finger into the slimy mixture and tasted it. "Perfectly perfect," he said. His tall wizard's hat wobbled on his head as he nodded. "Now pour it into your flasks and allow it to cool. Then all you have to do is drink it!"

"Mr. Jack," said Kate. "Do we have to drink it to make it work? Can't we just smell it? Or maybe dab a little on our shoes?"

"Oh, no," said Mr. Jack with a frown. "Potions are for drinking! And this is one of the easiest and most fun potions of all."

As Mr. Jack walked away, Kate and Whitney exchanged looks.

"I'm not sure I can do this," said Kate. "What if it tastes icky?"

"I'm pretty sure it will taste icky," replied Whitney. "Frog jelly? Grasshopper juice? It's going to taste awful. But, you only have to drink a little bit for the magic to work."

The girls followed Mr. Jack's instructions and carefully poured the purple goo into two flasks. Then, after the potions had cooled, Whitney and Kate each held a bottle of the potion.

"Well, here goes," said Whitney, shrugging. She closed her eyes and took a small sip of the potion.

"Eww. I can't look," said Kate, turning her head

away and scrunching her
eyes closed.

"Actually, it's not that
bad," said Whitney. "It kind
of tastes like grape juice!"

"Does it work?" asked
Kate, eyes wide.

"Let me try it out," said Whitney. She jumped,
but instead of just going up a little, she jumped all the
way to the ceiling! "Kate, it works!" she yelled. It was
like gravity didn't even exist anymore.

Kate smiled. It really did look fun. And now the
other students were trying the potion and experi-
encing the Uber Jumpy Rubbery Blubbery Power.
Girls were literally bouncing off the walls, just like
Mr. Jack had said. The room was full of laughter.

Kate wanted to join them. But then she looked
down at the potion. It was mostly purple but with
streaks of black and yellow. It looked slimy and gross.
She thought about the ingredients and shuddered
with disgust.

But Whitney had said the taste wasn't bad. She'd
said it tasted like grape juice. Kate brought the bottle
close to her face. She was planning on just smelling it,

but then she changed her mind. "Nope, nope, nope," she said. "I can't drink it."

Mr. Jack, who by now was also bouncing all around the room, bounced over to Kate. "Join us!" he cried. "Drink the potion!"

"Do I have to?"

"No, of course not! We would never make you drink something you don't want. You only have to learn how to make the potions to get a good grade. But drinking the potions is the fun part!"

"I don't want to," said Kate, wrinkling her nose.

"That's okay," said Mr. Jack with a warm smile. "Maybe next time."

He and the other students all held hands and jumped together. It looked as though the entire classroom was on one giant trampoline.

Kate felt sad that she couldn't join them. They were all having so much fun. But she couldn't drink the potion. Frog jelly? Bunny sweat? Grasshopper juice?

No.

She just couldn't do it.

CHAPTER 4
TASTER'S CHOICE

Every week, Mr. Jack taught Kate's class a new potion. Sometimes the recipes included ingredients that Kate was familiar with like honey, cinnamon, garlic, dandelion leaves, and peppermint. Sometimes they were ingredients she had heard of, but wasn't super familiar with like cod liver oil, campfire ash, and dead sea salt. Then there were the ingredients that she wished she'd never heard of, like coffin dust, snake scales, and worm spit.

Kate had always been a picky eater. She didn't like things like cheese or celery or tomatoes, but compared to the ingredients in Mr. Jack's potions, ordinary food seemed tame.

"I promise they don't taste bad," Whitney had told her.

But Kate still couldn't take a sip of the potions. "How can a potion with something called coffin dust *not* taste bad?" she wondered.

So even though Kate followed the recipes and made the potions perfectly, she missed out on x-ray vision, changing her skin color, super speed, and other fun things.

The rest of the class all drank the potion for magnetism and waved their hands over boxes of paper clips, giggling with delight as the paper clips would fly through the air like little metal bugs. Meanwhile, Kate sat off to the side with a sad look on her face, only watching.

The next week the rest of the class all drank the potion that allowed them to talk to animals. It was Bring Your Magic Pet to School Day, and so all the students were excited to finally speak with their pets. Whitney had a white ferret named Gabe.

"I keep asking him what he likes," said Whitney, "but he just keeps saying he's hungry. I've already fed him twice today."

Kate had brought Hop, her pet beta fish, to school. She really, really wanted to speak with Hop, but she eyed the green glowing potion and just knew it would taste awful.

"What's Hop got to say?" Mr. Jack asked her.

"I don't know," said Kate. "I didn't want to try the potion."

Mr. Jack looked at Hop and made a funny sound. Kate realized he was talking to her fish. "He says he likes you a lot."

Kate smiled. She was so glad that Hop liked her! But it would have been more fun if she'd heard Hop tell her himself. All day long the other students in Mr. Jack's class kept talking to their pets.

Kate had a dentist appointment that day, and she was glad to be picked up from school early.

"What's wrong?" her mom had asked as they drove to the dentist.

"I can't understand Hop," said Kate.

Kate's mom, who was not a witch, gave her a puzzled look.

"I don't like how the potions taste," Kate explained, even though technically she had never tried them.

Kate's mom still seemed a bit confused, but she nodded and told Kate she hoped she felt better later.

Week after week, Mr. Jack taught the class more fun potions. And week after week, Kate refused to drink the potions, and instead just watched while everyone else had fun. Julie and Bailey's teacher didn't teach as many potions because their teacher didn't have a witch's master degree in potions. Kate was beginning to wonder if she was in the wrong class after all.

CHAPTER 5
A NEW LESSON

At recess, Kate looked for Julie and Bailey to play hopscotch. But instead, she found them on their brooms playing a game of air tag. Kate got her broom and joined them. First, Bailey was it. She could fly really fast, and she quickly tagged Kate. Then Kate chased Julie on her broom. Julie looked behind her and when she saw Kate coming, she screamed playfully and tried to fly up, but she got confused and instead flew right into a tree!

Julie fell off her broom and gently floated to the ground.

"Oh, no!" Kate yelled. She flew down to the ground to check on her friend. "Are you okay?"

Julie stood up and brushed herself off. She giggled. "Yep, not hurt at all."

Kate was surprised to see Julie okay with falling. She knew her friend had an intense fear of heights.

Bailey joined Kate and Julie on the ground and jumped off her broom. "A few weeks ago you were scared to fly at all," Bailey said to Julie, "and now you can fly and fall and it doesn't bother you even a little bit."

"I had just made it up to be scarier in my mind than it was in real life," said Julie. "I know that it's okay to feel scared of things because that helps keep us safe. But my fear of flying had gotten a little out of control. I'm so glad I finally tried it."

Flying on her broomstick was another thing that Kate loved. She was really glad that Julie had been able to try flying so that the friends could all fly together.

"Hey Kate," said Bailey, "I heard that your class is learning a potion today to walk through walls."

"Yeah, we're learning it right after lunch," said Kate.

"I love Miss Betsy, but sometimes I wish we could learn more potions," said Bailey. "Will you tell me what it's like and maybe teach me the recipe?"

"I can teach you the recipe," said Kate, "but I won't be able to tell you what it's like."

"Why not?" asked Bailey.

"Oh, I don't drink the potions. Never. I don't like the way they taste," said Kate.

"I thought the potions always used a bit of magic to make them taste good," said Julie.

"That could be true," said Kate, "but I still know what ingredients are in the potion, and I know for a fact they are things I wouldn't like. Besides, people are always telling me normal foods like radishes and beef jerky taste good, but then I try them and I don't like them. I just don't like certain foods."

"So you really haven't tried any of the potions?" Bailey asked.

Kate shook her head.

"Not the one that made everyone bounce or the one to talk to pets or the one that made everyone's skin green?" Julie asked.

"I haven't tried any of them," said Kate.

"But maybe they don't all taste bad," said Bailey. "Maybe there's some you would like."

"I don't want to risk it," said Kate. "If I tried it and didn't like it, I'd probably throw up. I just don't like certain things. I think they're yucky."

Kate's friends said they understood, but something about the way they were acting made Kate think they felt sorry for her. The truth was that she really did feel sad about it, but what could she do? She couldn't help that she didn't like certain tastes. She couldn't help that she was more sensitive to flavors than the other students were.

CHAPTER 6
THE IMPOSSIBLE DECISION

Kate began to dislike the potion lessons. When Mr. Jack would announce the potion of the week, the other girls would cheer with excitement. But Kate knew she wouldn't get to do whatever fun thing the potion did, because she would never drink any of the potions. They were too gross.

So when Mr. Jack would talk about the planned potions, Kate would doodle in her notebook and think of her art projects back at home. She still liked Mr. Jack and Miss Annie's Magic School and the new friends she was making. She just didn't like potions, that's all there was to it. She could still grow up to be a good witch. She didn't have any problem *making* the potions. She only had a problem *drinking* the potions.

She could grow up to be a Master Wizard of Potions just like Mr. Jack, so long as she didn't have to test out the potions she made.

But then one day, Mr. Jack made an announcement about potions that changed everything.

Kate had hardly been listening. She was drawing a picture of a panda with a witch's hat chewing on a piece of bamboo.

Just then Whitney poked Kate in the arm with her wand, "Kate! Did you hear that?"

"Hear what?" said Kate. "A new potion? That's nice." She returned to her panda drawing.

"Not just any potion!" said Whitney. "This lets you paint pictures in the air with your fingertips!"

When her class had learned the potion that made them grow to be ten feet tall, Kate felt left out. When they learned the potion to make everything smell like roses, she felt kind of sad.

But now there was a potion involving art! How could Kate resist? She loved art. She thought about art all the time. It was her true passion. And now they were going to combine art and magic? It sounded like a dream come true.

After school that day, Kate went to speak with Mr. Jack. "Is it true the potion we're learning tomorrow will make it so we can paint in the air?"

"Hmm," said Mr. Jack tapping his chin. "Let me double-check that." He went to a shelf on his wall and pulled out a potion. "Yes, we're learning the Art-in-the-Air potion. Here it is." Mr. Jack took a sip. He offered it to Kate, but she shook her head.

"That's okay," said Mr. Jack. "It should start working now." He raised his index finger and began to draw in the air. As his finger moved, colors of red, yellow, green, blue, and purple appeared before him.

"A rainbow!" cried Kate.

Mr. Jack had drawn a rainbow that floated in the air. Kate looked at it from the front and then from the back.

"Here," said Mr. Jack, "you can have it."

He plucked the rainbow from the air and handed it to Kate. It was as light as a feather but as bright and pretty as a real rainbow.

"Cool!" said Kate.

"It's a rather fun spell for those who like art," said Mr. Jack. "Kate, aren't you an artist?"

"Yes, I am," said Kate. She held the rainbow out in front of her and let it go. It floated in the air again. Then Kate said, "Mr. Jack, may I see the recipe for the potion?"

Mr. Jack nodded and handed her a notecard. Kate looked at it. She was hoping that it would be something like graham crackers, chocolate, and marshmallows, which were all foods that she liked. However, that was the recipe for smores, not for making magical art. Instead, Kate read the card and found that they were all things that were colorful--but icky. Blue fungus, white spider silk, green mold, purple beet juice, red rosebuds, and the yellow yolk of a chicken egg. Eggs were something that Kate especially did not like.

Kate frowned.

"What's wrong?" asked Mr. Jack.

"I really, really want to try this potion, but these ingredients are disgusting," said Kate.

"But we're witches, wizards, and warlocks!" cried Mr. Jack in his excited way. "If we don't like how something tastes, we can use magic to make it taste better. It's already built into the recipe. That's why you have to follow the steps exactly and in the right order."

Kate looked at him doubtfully. "Spider silk, blue fungus, and eggs taste good together?"

"This potion tastes a little like strawberries," he said.

Kate scrunched up her nose.

"You don't believe me," asked Mr. Jack.

Kate shook her head.

"Then why don't you try it and see?" asked Mr. Jack.

"I'll think about it," said Kate. Then she left to find her friends.

CHAPTER 7
A TRICK

As Kate, Bailey, and Julie walked home that day, Kate told them all about the Art-in-the-Air potion and how badly she wanted to try it.

"I don't understand," said Bailey. "I thought strawberries were one of the few things you liked to eat."

"I do like strawberries," said Kate. "But there aren't any strawberries in the recipe. It's all gross stuff that I don't like. There's even eggs in this recipe."

"But didn't Mr. Jack say it would taste like strawberries?" Julie asked.

"Yeah, but adults try to get me to eat things I don't like all the time," said Kate. "My mom once told me broccoli tastes delicious. My dad said French onion soup was super-tasty. I tried them both and they were nasty-tasting. So, when Mr. Jack says the Art-in-the-Air potion tastes like strawberries, he's probably trying to trick me. Maybe he knows I like art and strawberries, and he thinks that might make me try it and that it will be worth it."

"Maybe it is worth it," said Bailey. "All these potions sound *really* cool."

Kate thought about it. Could she drink the potion even if it tasted really, really bad if it meant she'd get to do cool art?

Julie had overcome her fear of heights, and now she loved flying. Could Kate try something she didn't like and then grow to love it?

When she got home, she went back to her art easel to work on her latest painting--a tree with golden leaves. But Kate couldn't help thinking how cool it would be to paint the tree in the air, with branches and leaves going in all directions instead of having to be flat on the paper.

Plus, with the potion she could do any color. She pictured painting the tree with shimmering colors of purple and gold and green. It would take her art to a whole new level.

Kate thought about what it would be like to be in class tomorrow watching all the other students creating art while she just sat there. It wasn't fair! No one in class loved art as much as she did.

CHAPTER 8
A DECISION MADE

By the time Kate got to class, she had made up her mind. She would not drink the potion. She simply couldn't do it. It was all just too gross. Beet juice and eggs and spider silk could never taste like strawberries. She'd never even be able to swallow it. Just the thought of it made her feel a little sick.

Kate frowned as she and Whitney prepared the recipe. In fact, Kate was thinking about asking Mr. Jack if she might sit in his office or go to the library, so that she wouldn't feel left out when all of her classmates were making magical art together.

"I feel very sad for you, Kate," said Whitney. "I know how much you love art."

Kate nodded. She felt sad for herself, too.

"Maybe you could just take a small sip," said Whitney.

Kate shook her head. "No way. It would make me sick. I just know it."

"Okay," said Whitney. "No pressure. It's your choice."

When they finished the potion and poured it into the flasks, the liquid turned into a glittering rainbow hue that was always changing color.

After it had cooled, Whitney picked up the potion bottle. "Are you sure you don't want to try it?"

"Positive," said Kate.

Whitney shrugged and drank the potion.

"What's it taste like?" Kate asked.

"Like strawberries," said Whitney.

It was just like Mr. Jack had said, but still Kate couldn't think of drinking the potion.

"Do you at least want to pick what I draw?" Whitney asked.

Kate thought it was nice of Whitney to try to include her.

"How about a flower?" Kate suggested.

Whitney nodded. She waved her hands around in front of her and colors of pink and red and orange appeared as she created a magical painting in the air.

Kate thought the flower was beautiful. She even told Whitney that. But Kate really, really wanted to make one of these magical art creations herself.

She picked up the potion bottle and looked into the opening. The potion bubbled magically with every color imaginable. Then she set the bottle down.

Whitney noticed and turned to her. "What are you doing?" she asked.

Kate bit her lip. "I was thinking about trying it. But I can't."

All around the room, students were drawing horses, houses, mountains, and mermaids. The drawings weren't flat, like those drawn on a piece of paper. The drawings were 3-D! And the colors weren't just red, yellow, blue, and green, like the colors in a box of crayons. The magical 3-D drawings were of any color the students could imagine. Sparkly yellowish-green, glittering deep purple, shining bright silver, and amazing amber-gold.

Kate picked up the bottle. "I'll do it. I'll drink the potion. I have to!"

"Really?" Whitney asked in surprise.

Kate nodded.

Whitney nodded, too. "You can do it, Kate!"

Kate took a deep breath, plugged her nose, squeezed her eyes shut, and chugged the potion down before she could change her mind.

When she had swallowed the entire potion, she set the bottle down. Her eyes were wide and frightened.

Then Kate gagged. She gagged as if she had just drank a bucket full of nasty muddy swamp water, or a big jug of rotten milk. Next, she coughed. Her tongue shot out of her mouth. Her eyes watered. She coughed and sputtered.

"It's disgusting!" cried Kate. "Blegh! Yuck! Ick! Gross! Disgusting!"

"Are you all right?" said Whitney, leaving her flower drawing and coming to Kate's side.

"No!" shouted Kate. She fell down on the floor and kicked her feet. "I'm sick! I feel awful! Get me to the nurse's office!"

Mr. Jack came over. "What's the matter, girls? What's wrong?"

Kate sputtered and gagged and rolled on the floor. Some of the other girls also turned to see what the matter was.

"Kate!" said Mr. Jack, "What happened? Are you all right?"

"No!" shouted Kate again, holding her stomach and kicking her feet. "And I'll never drink another potion ever again!"

CHAPTER 9
ALL IN HER HEAD

Kate wasn't taken to the nurse's office. Kate was so sure that the potion would taste bad that she thought it really was bad. But it wasn't bad. Just as Mr. Jack and Whitney and everyone else said, it tasted nice. Like strawberries. After a few moments, Kate realized that the bad taste was just in her head. And in another moment or two after that, she realized she'd been all wrong.

"Wait," said Kate. She stood up. "Wait, no. It didn't taste bad at all. It really did taste like strawberries."

By this time all the other students had also gathered around Kate.

Mr. Jack said, "Go on, Kate. Tell us what happened."

"Hmm," said Kate. She was amazed. A smile came to her face. "I thought it tasted really disgusting, but it was only my imagination. It really tasted good. Like strawberries. No, that's not quite right. The potion tasted like a strawberry smoothie! It wasn't nasty! It was delicious!"

Mr. Jack and the other students laughed and clapped and cheered. They'd been having so much fun with the potions. They knew Kate was a picky eater, and they felt sad that Kate wasn't able to join in the good times. But now they knew she could, and they were glad for her.

Kate brushed herself off, shook her head, and smiled. "How could those weird ingredients end up tasting so nice?" she asked.

Mr. Jack patted Kate on the arm and said, "You know how."

"Magic!" said Kate.

"That's right," said Mr. Jack. "And now," he added, "back to your art, students! I want you all to create the most fabulous creations for your rooms and your parents and your friends!"

Kate didn't waste another moment. Magical art was all she wanted to do now. She wanted to paint the magical tree that she'd been imagining. And so she began. The rest of the class seemed unable to return to their own projects. As Kate painted colorful stroke after stroke and the tree took shape, the rest of the class had to watch.

Even Mr. Jack was impressed. Kate first painted the tree's trunk. It was tall and silver, and it climbed and twisted into the air. Next, Kate drew the leaves, each one perfectly detailed. The colors Kate chose and the shadows she sketched made it seem like bright summer sunshine was beaming down onto the tree.

The leaves shimmered. Kate added budding flowers to the tree, and to tend the flowers she drew large bumble bees with shiny wings and fuzzy black and yellow bodies.

When she'd finished, Kate stepped back to look at it.

"Kate," said Whitney. "It's beautiful!"

The other students in the classroom agreed. They said, "Wow!" "Stunning!" "Incredible!"

Mr. Jack strolled around the silver trunk of the tree and looked up through the branches and leaves. He plucked one of the bumble bees from the drawing and admired it.

"Such wondrous colors and clever shading!" he said. Then he set the bee back on its flower. "Kate, in all my years of teaching, I've never seen an art project quite like this."

"Are you glad you gave that potion a try?" asked Whitney.

"I sure am," said Kate.

CHAPTER 10
ONE LITTLE TASTE

After that, Kate always tried the potions they made. At least she always tried one small sip.

Sometimes she didn't like the taste at all, and when that happened, she wouldn't drink anymore.

But more often, she found that she didn't mind the taste and a lot of the times she even liked it! She didn't have to miss out on the magic the potions created in Mr. Jack's class anymore. She tried new things, even though it sometimes scared her.

At home, Kate's mom was surprised to see her daughter trying more foods, too.

"If I can eat spider silk, I can eat brussels sprouts," said Kate.

Kate even invited her friends Bailey and Julie over to try some new foods.

Kate still didn't like eggs. And she never got used to the taste of frog jelly. But she discovered that she really liked pumpkin, witches' stew, and bat wings, even though she never would have guessed it before.

"I think it's kind of like when I was scared to fly," said Julie. "Mostly it was just my mind telling me it was going to be bad."

"Exactly," said Kate. "I let my brain tell me things would taste gross without letting my tongue do the tasting!"

Kate was happy to have discovered many new

flavors that she loved, but most of all, she was happy to have joined her love of art with her love of magic.

After their taste-test, Kate painted a picture of herself with her friends and then they all stood together to admire it.

"Now that is beautiful," said Bailey.

Kate smiled. "It really is."

PLEASE LEAVE A REVIEW

Thank you for reading this book. We hope you enjoyed it! We would really appreciate it if you would please take a moment to review *Kate: A Magic School for Girls Chapter Book* on Amazon or other retail sites. Thank you!

WWW.AMLUZZADER.COM

- blog
- freebies
- newsletter
- contact info

OTHER BOOKS BY
A.M. Luzzader

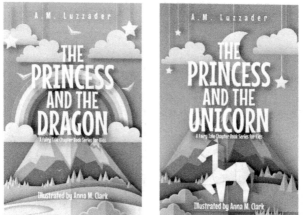

A Fairy Tale Chapter Book Series for Kids

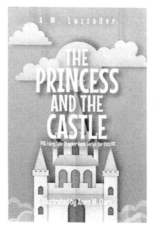

For ages
6-8

OTHER BOOKS BY
A.M. Luzzader

A Mermaid in Middle Grade
Books 1-3

For ages
8-12

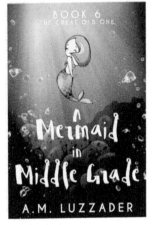

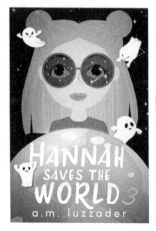

A.M. Luzzader is an award-winning children's author who writes chapter books and middle grade books. She specializes in writing books for preteens. A.M.'s fantasy adventure series 'A Mermaid in Middle Grade' is a magical coming of age book series for ages 8-12. She is also the author of the 'Hannah Saves the

World' series, which is a children's mystery adventure, also for ages 8-12.

A.M. decided she wanted to write fun stories for kids when she was still a kid herself. By the time she was in fourth grade, she was already writing short stories. In fifth grade, she bought a typewriter at a garage sale to put her words into print, and in sixth grade she added illustrations. Now that she has decided what she wants to be when she grows up, A.M. writes books for girls and boys full time. She was selected as the Writer of the Year in 2019-2020 by the League of Utah Writers.

A.M. is the mother of a 10-year-old and a 13-year-old who often inspire her stories. She lives with her husband and children in northern Utah. She is a devout cat person and avid reader.

A.M. Luzzader's books are appropriate for ages 5-12. Her chapter books are intended for kindergarten to third grade, and her middle grade books are for third grade through sixth grade. Find out more about A.M., sign up to receive her newsletter, and get special offers at her website: www.amluzzader.com.

 facebook.com/a.m.luzzader

amazon.com/author/amluzzader

ABOUT THE ILLUSTRATOR

Anna Hilton is sixteen years old and has lived in Utah all of her life. She enjoys art, dancing, and spending time with her friends. Anna loves to read novels and to draw pictures of everything she sees.

Made in the USA
Monee, IL
19 September 2021

78390681R00049